The Alpha Firefighter

A Protective Alpha Fated Mates
Steamy Omegaverse Romance

Ash Jade

D ear Reader,

Welcome to Sanctuary, a hidden mountain town whispered about in the wider omegaverse, a place where worn-down omegas come to heal and alphas learn that strength is measured in gentleness, not dominance. If you've made it this far, maybe part of you is curious... or hopeful... or simply ready to step into a world where instinct doesn't have to hurt, and where every story bends toward safety, connection, and a well-earned happily-ever-after.

Here, the omegaverse works a little differently.

Alphas, betas, and omegas still move through life guided by pheromones, instincts, and bonds, but Sanctuary is a refuge, one carved out of grief, rebuilt with stubborn hope, and held together by a pack that refuses to let anyone fall through the cracks. Heats and ruts still come like wild weather, but they're met with care, consent, and hands that steady instead of seize. And sometimes, the mountain air carries something more ancient still: the pull of fated mates, that quiet click inside your chest when you realize home might be a person as much as a place.

Each novella in this series is a fast, high-heat, heart-forward escape. A story about a protective alpha, a brave omega, and the slow re-teaching of trust. You can read them in order or wander in wherever you like. Every couple stands alone, yet each book threads another stitch into the found-family tapestry of Sanctuary.

Before you step inside, a few gentle warnings:

These stories contain explicit sexual content, primal dynamics, instinct-driven tension, and adult themes. They are not dark romance, but they *do* explore trauma recovery, vulnerability, and the process of learning to choose yourself again. Please honor your comfort level and step away if something doesn't sit right with you.

Additional content considerations: violence, injury, death, mentions of sexual violence (not depicted but discussed), and themes of healing from past harm.

If Sanctuary sounds like somewhere you might want to linger—if you're ready for protective alphas, fierce omegas, small-town gossip, soft pack dinners, and bonds that bloom where hurt once lived—then settle in.

The mountains are waiting.

— Ash Jade

Contents

1

The smoke claws its way into my lungs before I'm even fully awake. I jolt upright in bed, my throat closing, eyes stinging. Red-orange light dances across my bedroom walls—wrong, wrong, wrong. Not sunrise. Fire. My rental house is burning, and I'm trapped inside.

I fumble for my phone, dropping it twice before my fingers close around it. The screen reads 3:47 AM. Three missed calls from the hospital where my shift starts in four hours. They'll have to find another nurse.

Smoke billows under my door in thick, angry tendrils. I press my sleeve against my mouth, coughing until my ribs ache.

"Think, Avery," I rasp to myself. "Move."

I grab my scrub top from the floor, wet it in the bathroom sink, and press it over my nose and mouth. The water feels impossibly cold against the growing inferno outside my bedroom.

The hallway door handle burns my palm when I touch it. Basic fire safety—check before opening.

The flames must be in the living room already. My tiny rental has only two exits: front door through the living room, back door through the kitchen. I drag my comforter off the bed, wrap it around my shoulders over my sleep shorts and tank top, and edge toward my bedroom window.

It sticks, warped from years of mountain humidity. I throw my weight against it and feel something in my shoulder give way. The pain shoots white–hot down my arm, but the window doesn't budge.

The smoke thickens. My vision swims.

My lungs spasm with each breath, like someone's wringing them out. I'm a nurse—I know exactly what smoke inhalation does to a body. How long I have. How it will feel when my airways swell shut.

The curtains near my door ignite. Flames lick across the ceiling, consuming the cheap popcorn texture. No way out now.

I slide down against the wall beneath my window. Some clinical part of my brain notes my racing pulse, the thundering of my omega instincts screaming danger, danger, run. But there's nowhere to run.

My eyelids grow heavy. Black spots dance across my vision like malicious fireflies. Sweat drips down my spine, mixing with the tears streaking through the soot on my cheeks.

So this is how I die. Not from my father's controlling pack. Not from a hospital pathogen. Just ordinary fire in an ordinary town where I thought I'd finally found sanctuary.

A crash echoes from somewhere far away. Male voices. Heavy footsteps. Probably hallucinations as my oxygen-starved brain fails.

Then my bedroom door splinters inward, and a figure materializes through the smoke—massive, helmeted, masked. My oxygen-deprived mind registers only: alpha. The awareness hits my bloodstream like adrenaline.

He moves toward me with purpose, kneels beside me. "I've got you," he says, voice muffled by his mask but somehow still cutting through the roar of the flames. "Stay with me."

I try to speak, but only coughing emerges. He doesn't hesitate—just scoops me up against his chest like I weigh nothing. One arm under my knees, the other supporting my back. The pain in my shoulder flares, but it feels distant now.

He turns and carries me through the inferno that was my bedroom door. The heat is unbearable a physical wall we push through. I curl into his chest, face pressed against the rough material of his turnout coat. Even through the smoke and burning plastic, I catch his scent—pine, woodsmoke, mountain air. Something inside me stirs in response, a recognition I'm too delirious to understand.

"Almost there," he murmurs, his pace quickening. The floor groans beneath us. Embers rain down from what remains of the ceiling. He hunches over me, shielding my body with his.

Then we're outside. The cool night air slams into my lungs like a fist. I gasp, choking, sucking in precious oxygen between wracking coughs. He strides across my tiny yard, away from the hungry flames consuming everything I own. My vision clears enough to see neighbors gathered in their pajamas, firetrucks with flashing lights, hoses snaking across the street.

My rescuer stops by an ambulance, hesitating before setting me down on the gurney. I clutch at his jacket, suddenly terrified to let go. He gently pries my fingers loose, but doesn't move away.

"You're safe now," he says, and finally removes his mask.

Our eyes meet. His are amber-gold in the firelight, pupils dilated. Something electric passes between us—a current, a connection that makes my breath catch for reasons entirely unrelated to smoke inhalation.

He inhales sharply, nostrils flaring. And I know he feels it too. The unmistakable tug of alpha to omega. The recognition that slams through both our bodies like a physical blow.

"Ethan! We need you on the south side!" Another firefighter calls.

He blinks, breaking our gaze. "I'm Ethan. Ethan Rawlins."

"Avery," I manage between coughs. "Avery Chen."

His expression shifts—something primal flashing across his features before he controls it. "You're in good hands, Avery. I'll check on you after."

A paramedic bustles over, fixing an oxygen mask over my face. Ethan backs away, his eyes never leaving mine until he turns to jog back toward the burning house.

"Vitals?" the paramedic asks, pressing fingers to my wrist.

"I'm a nurse," I rasp, pointlessly.

"Then you know to shut up and breathe."

I obey, watching over the oxygen mask as my entire life burns to the ground. Eight months in Sanctuary, rebuilding after escaping my father's pack. All my possessions, nursing textbooks, the few photos I'd managed to take when I fled. The independence I'd clawed out for myself—gone in minutes.

Tears stream down my face, cutting clean trails through the soot. The paramedic checks my shoulder, pronouncing it only strained, not dislocated. Small mercies.

Through the crowd and smoke, I catch glimpses of Ethan working. His movements are precise, controlled. But every few minutes, his gaze finds me across the chaos, as if he's physically incapable of not checking that I'm still there.

I should find this creepy. Instead, something deep in my omega hindbrain purrs with satisfaction.

"Are you on any medications? Any history of respiratory issues?" the paramedic asks, pulling me back to reality.

"No. Just… I have nowhere to go now." The words come out small and pathetic.

The paramedic squeezes my uninjured shoulder. "This is Sanctuary, honey. We take care of our own."

But I'm not one of their own. I'm just a drifter who thought she'd found a hiding place. The weight of that truth settles in my chest, heavier than the smoke damage to my lungs.

Across the yard, Ethan stiffens and turns to stare at me again, as if he heard my thoughts. His expression is fierce, determined—possessive in a way that should send me running. Instead, I can't look away.

In the midst of losing everything, I've found something I wasn't looking for. Something I've spent my entire life running from.

My fated mate.

2

Dawn breaks over the smoldering remains of my rental. The paramedic finally stops hovering, leaving me wrapped in a shock blanket on the back step of the ambulance. My throat feels scraped raw, each breath a deliberate effort. Everything I own is either ash or water-damaged beyond salvation. The fire chief confirmed what I already suspected—electrical fire, started in the walls. Nothing I could have done. Small comfort when you're sitting in borrowed sweatpants with nowhere to go.

I clutch the paper cup of lukewarm coffee someone pressed into my hands an hour ago. It tastes like ash—everything does. My phone is gone. My wallet. My nursing credentials. My car keys were hanging by the front door, which means my car is just a useless hunk of metal in the driveway until I can get replacements.

A tall, broad-shouldered man approaches—the sheriff, based on his uniform.

"Miss Chen?" His voice is gentler than his appearance suggests. "I'm Sheriff Jake Rawlins. How are you holding up?"

"I've been better." My attempt at a smile feels like a grimace.

He nods, hands resting on his belt. "We've got a few options for you. The community center has emergency beds, or there's Marge's Motel down on Main. The department has a voucher system for situations like this."

My stomach knots. Public charity. Being indebted. Visible, vulnerable. Everything I've avoided since fleeing my father's pack.

"Thank you." I force the words past my pride. "The motel sounds—"

"She'll stay with me."

The voice comes from behind us. Ethan, still in his turnout gear minus the helmet, face streaked with soot, amber eyes locked on mine. He's showered at some point—his dark hair is damp, curling at his neck—but still smells of smoke and something uniquely him that makes my omega sit up and take notice.

"Ethan," Jake says in a warning tone, "maybe Miss Chen would prefer—"

"I have a spare room." Ethan's jaw sets stubbornly, gaze never leaving mine. "It's sitting empty. No sense in her taking up space at the shelter or wasting money at Marge's."

The two men, who definitely look related, have a silent standoff. I watch, feeling increasingly like furniture being argued over.

"It's not the department's call," I interrupt, straightening my spine. "Or yours. It's mine."

Ethan's expression softens fractionally. "Of course it is. But the offer stands."

I should say no. Everything about this screams danger—not physical danger, but the risk of dependence, of owing an alpha, of proximity to someone who makes my scent receptors go haywire. The problem is, he's right. The practical choice is obvious.

"Just until I can make other arrangements," I say, hating how small my voice sounds. "A day or two at most."

Relief flashes across Ethan's face before he controls his expression. Jake looks between us, eyebrows raised.

"Your call," he tells me, then turns to his brother. "Ethan, a word?"

They step aside, speaking in low tones. I don't try to eavesdrop, focusing instead on the smoldering remains of my independence. The firefighters are still dousing hot spots, but it's clear nothing is salvageable. Eight months of carefully constructed life, gone overnight.

When Ethan returns, he's carrying a department duffel bag. "Spare clothes. They'll be huge on you, but better than what the hospital donated."

I take the bag, our fingers brushing. The contact sends a shock up my arm that I stubbornly ignore. "Thanks."

"My truck's over there." He points to a battered blue pickup. "Whenever you're ready."

The paramedic clears me to leave after a final vitals check and strict instructions to rest my lungs. Ethan waits nearby, giving me space but clearly unwilling to go far. When I stand, my legs tremble. He steps forward as if to catch me, then forces himself to stop when I straighten.

The drive through town is quiet. Sanctuary is just waking up, bakery lights glowing against the early morning gray. I stare out the window, watching the small mountain town slip past. Eight months here, and it still feels foreign. A way station, not a home.

"You work at the hospital?" Ethan breaks the silence.

"ER nurse. Night shift, usually."

He nods. "Jake mentioned you moved here earlier this year."

"Eight months ago." I don't elaborate.

Ethan taps his fingers on the steering wheel. "I've only been back six months myself. Was with a wildfire team down in Colorado before that."

This pulls my attention from the window. "Back?"

"Grew up here. Left when I was eighteen." His voice tightens. "Needed space from..." He trails off, then shrugs. "Family expectations. Jake followed our dad into law enforcement. Everyone assumed I would too."

"But you chose fire instead."

A ghost of a smile touches his lips. "Poetic, isn't it?"

Something in his tone makes me think there's more to the story, but I don't press. We're nearing the edge of town, the buildings giving way to pine forest. Ethan turns onto a narrow dirt road that winds upward.

"You live far out," I observe.

"Like my privacy." His knuckles whiten on the steering wheel. "Jake's in town proper. Good for the sheriff to be accessible. I prefer quiet."

I understand the subtext. Distance from his brother. Space from whatever complex family dynamics drove him away for years. I respect that. I've got plenty of my own demons I keep at arm's length.

The truck rounds a curve, and his cabin comes into view. It's not what I expected—not some bachelor disaster or primitive hunting lodge. It's modest but well-maintained. Two stories with a wide front porch, garden beds along the front, a detached garage to the side. Solar panels glint on the south-facing roof.

"It's nice," I say, surprised by how much I mean it.

Ethan parks, then hurries around to open my door before I can. The gesture feels oddly formal, at odds with his rugged appearance. I slide out, careful not to brush against him, the duffel clutched to my chest like a shield.

Inside, the cabin smells like him—pine, woodsmoke, alpha. My omega instincts recognize it instantly as safe, which just makes me more determined to keep my guard up.

"Kitchen, living room," he says, gesturing awkwardly. "Bathroom downstairs here. My bedroom's upstairs, and the spare room's up there too."

I follow him up the wooden staircase, noting the lack of personal touches. No family photos. Minimal decoration. The space of someone who exists here but doesn't quite live here.

The spare room is small but clean. Plain navy bedding, empty dresser, window overlooking the forest. He's cleared space in the closet, I notice. As if he's been preparing for someone.

"I'll get you some towels," he says, hovering in the doorway. "Bathroom up here connects to both rooms, but I'll use the one downstairs while you're here."

"You don't have to—"

"I want to." His voice leaves no room for argument. "You need space."

Something inside me uncoils slightly. He's giving me territory. An alpha ceding ground to an omega in his own home.

"Thank you," I say, meaning it this time.

"There's food in the fridge. Help yourself." He backs away, then stops. "I'm off shift for three days. I can drive you to the hospital to sort out your paperwork. Or to get clothes. Whatever you need."

I swallow hard against the sudden tightness in my throat. Kindness is more devastating than cruelty sometimes. "I'll figure it out."

"I know you will." And the way he says it—not condescending, but certain—catches me off guard. "I'll be downstairs if you need anything."

After he leaves, I sit on the edge of the bed, the duffel beside me. The room feels safe in a way I can't articulate. I should be planning my next move, figuring out insurance claims and replacement IDs. Instead, exhaustion crashes over me in waves.

I curl up on top of the covers, still in the borrowed clothes, and close my eyes. Just for a minute, I tell myself. Just until I have the strength to rebuild my walls and remember all the reasons I can't stay here.

Sleep takes me before I can talk myself out of it.

3

—·—

I wake to unfamiliar shadows on the ceiling, heart hammering before memory returns. Fire. Smoke. Strong arms carrying me to safety. Ethan Rawlins and his spare room. I blink away the disorientation, my body sinking into the softness of a bed that isn't mine because I don't have one anymore. The enormity of my loss crashes over me in waves—not just possessions but security, independence, the careful distance I've maintained from everyone since arriving in Sanctuary.

Sunlight streams through curtains I don't recognize. The clock on the nightstand reads 2:17 PM. I've slept nearly eight hours, my body demanding recovery after the night's trauma. My throat still burns with each breath, a constant reminder.

Someone has been in the room while I slept—a folded stack of clothes sits on the dresser with a note. The handwriting is blocky, decisive.

Grabbed these from the general store. Receipt's there if anything needs exchanging. Bathroom's all yours. -E

The clothes are simple—jeans, t-shirts, a hoodie, underwear still in packages. All in my size. I try not to think about Ethan Rawlins buying me underwear, or how he knew my size just by looking at me. Alpha intuition, or something more unsettling?

The bathroom is spotlessly clean, as if recently scrubbed. Two fluffy towels wait on the counter beside new toiletries—shampoo, conditioner, soap, toothbrush, even face wash. Nothing fancy, all practical, but the thoughtfulness catches me off guard.

I shower until the hot water loosens my stiff muscles, washing away soot I hadn't even realized was still clinging to my skin. The soap smells like pine—like him. I try not to dwell on that as I dress in the new clothes, which fit perfectly.

The stairs creak under my feet as I descend. Ethan stands at the stove, his back to me, shoulders broad beneath a faded t-shirt. He's cooking something that smells like heaven to my empty stomach.

"You don't have to feed me too," I say from the doorway.

He turns, spatula in hand, eyes widening slightly as they take me in. Something flickers across his face—approval, possession, hunger—before he masks it.

"Figured you'd be starving." His voice is deliberately casual. "Eggs okay? I've got bacon too."

My stomach growls in response, embarrassingly loud in the quiet kitchen. The corner of his mouth twitches. "I'll take that as a yes."

I hover awkwardly until he nods toward the small kitchen table. "Sit. Coffee's ready."

The domesticity of it all feels dangerous, more intimate than it should. I pour myself coffee from the carafe, adding a splash of cream from the tiny pitcher he's set out. Like we're playing house.

"Thank you," I manage, wrapping my hands around the warm mug. "For the clothes. And everything else."

He shrugs, sliding eggs onto plates. "Least I could do."

"Most people would say pulling me from a burning building was plenty."

His jaw tightens. "You needed help. I could provide it." As if it's that simple.

We eat in awkward silence for a few minutes. The food is good—simple but well-prepared. Ethan eats methodically, his movements controlled like everything else about him.

"How's the shoulder?" he asks eventually.

I rotate it experimentally. "Sore, but functional."

He nods. "Hospital gave me your medication schedule. Next dose of anti-inflammatories in about an hour."

The fact that he knows this, that he's tracking my medical needs, should bother me. Instead, something warm unfurls in my chest. "You don't have to babysit me."

"Not babysitting. Just..." He struggles for words. "Being thorough."

I take a sip of coffee to hide my expression. "Have you always been a firefighter?"

The question seems to catch him off guard. "Since I was twenty. Drove Jake crazy when I chose fire instead of law enforcement."

"Why did you?"

His fork pauses halfway to his mouth. No one's asked him this before, I realize.

"Fire doesn't lie," he says finally. "It doesn't have ulterior motives. It just is. You fight it on its terms, nothing political about it."

"Unlike being sheriff."

"Unlike being anything in a small town when you're a Rawlins." His voice carries years of weight. "Jake thrives on it. I don't."

I understand more than he knows. "And yet you came back."

Something vulnerable flashes in his eyes. "Family's still family. Dad died last year. Massive heart attack. Jake needed… well, he didn't need help, but he needed someone who understood."

"I'm sorry about your father."

He shrugs, but the casualness feels forced. "We weren't close. But thanks." He clears his throat. "What about you? Always been a nurse?"

"Since I was twenty-two." I don't elaborate on what drove me to a profession built on caring for others when no one had ever properly cared for me. "ER work keeps me on my toes."

He studies me with those amber eyes. "And before Sanctuary? Where was home?"

My fork clatters against the plate. "Nowhere worth mentioning."

To his credit, he doesn't push. Just nods and changes the subject. "I need to go into town for supplies. You probably need things too—replacement ID, clothes that aren't from the general store."

"I can't impose—"

"It's not an imposition if I'm going anyway." His tone leaves little room for argument. "Unless you'd rather stay here and rest more."

The thought of being alone in his space, surrounded by his scent, is more unsettling than the alternative. "I'll come."

The drive into town feels different in daylight. Sanctuary unfolds along the mountain base—Main Street lined with century-old buildings, newer developments tucked behind. People wave as Ethan's truck passes, their curious gazes lingering when they spot me in the passenger seat.

"Small town," he explains, noticing my discomfort. "News travels fast. Everyone knows about the fire by now."

"Great." Just what I need—more attention.

"They're not judging. They're concerned." He pulls into a parking spot outside the town hall. "Sanctuary takes care of its own."

"I'm not one of their own."

He gives me a long look. "You might be surprised."

Inside the town hall, a friendly beta clerk helps me start the process for replacement identification. Ethan hovers nearby, not interfering but present, as if his alpha instincts won't let him stray too far. I should find it suffocating. Instead, it's oddly comforting.

"Ethan Rawlins, as I live and breathe!" A female voice cuts through the quiet. "Since when do you voluntarily come to town hall?"

A petite woman with honey-blonde hair approaches, her smile warm. She's beautiful in an effortless way, but it's her scent that catches my attention—omega, like me, but paired with something else. Mated.

"Emma," Ethan nods, his posture relaxing slightly. "Just helping out."

Her curious gaze shifts to me. "And you must be Avery. I heard about the fire. I'm Emma Rawlins, Jake's wife."

"Nice to meet you," I manage, surprised by her friendliness.

"I've brought some things for you." She gestures to a tote bag I hadn't noticed. "Clothes, toiletries, a spare phone charger. We're about the same size."

My throat tightens with unexpected emotion. "That's... really kind of you."

"That's Sanctuary," she says simply, then turns to Ethan with narrowed eyes. "Are you feeding her properly?"

He rolls his eyes. "Yes, Emma."

"Good. Because if not, you're both coming to dinner tonight." She says it like a threat, but her smile is genuine.

"We couldn't impose—" I begin.

"Nonsense. You've had a trauma, and this one—" she jerks her thumb at Ethan, "—isn't exactly known for his social graces."

"We ate breakfast," he protests.

Emma laughs, the sound bright in the stuffy office. "Wow, breakfast. Give the man a medal." She turns back to me. "Seriously though, if you need anything—a listening ear, a place to stay that isn't with this grumpy bear, whatever—I'm here."

The offer feels genuine, not the polite small-town platitudes I expected. "Thank you."

After Emma leaves, promising to call later, I turn to find Ethan watching me with an odd expression.

"What?" I ask.

"Nothing." He shakes his head. "It's just... Emma doesn't warm up to people easily. She must see something special in you."

I don't know how to respond to that. The clerk saves me by returning with forms to sign.

As we leave town hall, I find myself noticing Sanctuary differently—the café owner sweeping her sidewalk waves to us, a group of schoolchildren run past laughing, an elderly man tips his hat to Ethan with a respectful nod.

"Small towns," I murmur.

"Good and bad," Ethan agrees. "No privacy, but no one falls through the cracks either."

I think about my eight months here, keeping to myself, working nights, barely interacting. I'd chosen Sanctuary for its name, not its reality. Maybe I've been missing something.

Ethan's hand hovers near the small of my back as we navigate a crowded sidewalk, not quite touching but present. Every instinct I've cultivated since escaping my father screams danger at the proximity of an alpha showing protective behaviors.

But beneath those learned warnings, something deeper and more primal purrs in satisfaction. Something I've spent years silencing suddenly wants to be heard.

And that terrifies me more than any fire ever could.

4

— · —

Three days slip by in a strange, suspended reality. Ethan and I orbit each other carefully in the cabin, maintaining polite distance while my scent gradually permeates his space and his mine. I take the couch when he's at the station for his shift, unable to settle in the bedroom that doesn't smell enough of him. I cook dinner when he's due home, telling myself it's just repayment for his hospitality. We don't talk about what happened in those first moments when he carried me from the fire—that instant, visceral recognition that hums between us whenever we're in the same room.

The hospital grants me emergency leave with pay—a kindness I didn't expect. My insurance claim moves forward with surprising efficiency, probably helped along by Sheriff Jake's influence. Emma brings me more clothes, drags me to coffee, introduces me to people. For the first time since arriving in Sanctuary, I find myself becoming visible.

It's terrifying.

I'm helping Ethan unload groceries from his truck when I first sense something wrong. The hair on the back of my neck stands up. A car drives past the general store too slowly, out-of-state plates, tinted windows. Not a tourist vehicle.

"What is it?" Ethan asks, instantly alert to my tension.

I shake my head. "Nothing." But I hurry inside with the bags, instinctively seeking shelter.

That night, I dream of my father's house—the oppressive weight of alpha command in every room, the careful cataloguing of suitable alpha matches for his omega daughter, the suffocating sensation of being property rather than person. I wake gasping, sheets tangled around my legs.

Ethan appears in the doorway, shirtless and rumpled with sleep, eyes sharp with concern. "Avery?"

"Just a dream." I push damp hair from my face. "I'm fine."

He hesitates, clearly wanting to come closer, to comfort. Instead, he nods once. "I'll make tea."

I find him in the kitchen, two steaming mugs waiting. Neither of us mentions the hour—3:17 AM—or why he responded so instantly to my distress. We sip in companionable silence until the tightness in my chest eases.

The next day, Emma convinces me to join her for lunch at Marge's Diner. The bell jingles as we enter, and the usual hum of conversation dips then resumes. I follow Emma to a booth, keeping my back to the wall—old habits.

"Jake says your insurance came through," Emma says, scanning the menu she surely knows by heart.

"Yeah. Enough for a security deposit on a new place, at least." The words catch in my throat. The thought of leaving Ethan's cabin shouldn't make me feel this hollow.

Emma studies me over her menu. "No rush, you know. Ethan's place has been too empty since he came back."

Before I can respond, the diner's door swings open. Two men enter—one tall and lean, the other stockier with a military buzz cut. Both alphas. Both wearing the same expression of cold calculation as they scan the room.

My blood freezes in my veins. I know them. Not personally, but I recognize the insignia on their leather jackets—my father's pack symbol. Scouts.

Emma notices my reaction instantly. "Avery? What's wrong?"

The taller one spots me, nudges his companion. They approach our booth with predatory confidence.

"Avery Chen." Not a question. "You've led us on quite a chase."

I grip the edge of the table to stop my hands from shaking. "I don't know you."

"No, but your father sends his regards." The stockier one smiles without warmth. "It's time to come home, omega."

Emma straightens beside me. "Excuse me, but you're interrupting our lunch."

They ignore her completely. "Your father has been patient. Three years is long enough for this little... independence experiment."

My throat closes with familiar panic—the same choking fear I felt in the fire, but worse because this cage has been following me my entire life.

"I'm not going anywhere," I manage. "I left the pack. I'm not bound to it."

The taller one leans forward, voice dropping to a hiss. "Pack bonds are for life. Your father's claim supersedes all others. You're pack property until properly mated to an alpha of his choosing."

"She's not property."

The voice comes from behind them, low and dangerous. Ethan stands in the diner's entrance, still in his uniform from the station, eyes blazing. The entire diner falls silent.

The scouts turn, assessing him with narrowed eyes. "This doesn't concern you, firefighter."

"It absolutely concerns me." Ethan moves closer, every line of his body radiating controlled fury.

"You're harassing a citizen of Sanctuary on private property."

"We're collecting what belongs to our pack alpha." The stocky one sneers. "Pack law supersedes your backwater town ordinances."

Ethan's hands clench at his sides. "Nothing and no one in this town belongs to anyone. Especially not Avery."

The taller scout sniffs the air, eyes widening slightly. "Ah. I see. You've developed an interest in the alpha's daughter. I'm afraid you're too late. She's promised elsewhere."

"I'm promised nowhere," I snap, finding my voice. "I left. I'm not going back."

"Your father anticipated this response." The stocky one reaches inside his jacket, producing an official-looking document. "This is a pack court order declaring you incompetent to make your own decisions due to omega instability. We're authorized to return you by any means necessary."

Emma gasps beside me. I feel the blood drain from my face.

Ethan takes another step forward, and something in his scent shifts—deepens, sharpens. The scouts instinctively back up.

"I suggest," Ethan says, each word precise and deadly calm, "that you take your paper and leave. Now."

"Or what?" The taller one regains his composure. "You'll make us? You're outnumbered, fireman."

"Actually," comes another voice, "he's not."

Sheriff Jake Rawlins stands in the doorway, hand resting casually on his holster. Behind him, several deputies and what appears to be half the town's male population linger on the sidewalk.

"This is a pack matter—" the stocky scout begins.

"This is my jurisdiction," Jake interrupts. "And in my jurisdiction, we don't recognize pack claims on individuals against their will." He steps forward, hand extended. "The document, please."

Reluctantly, the scout hands it over. Jake scans it, then folds it neatly and tucks it into his pocket.

"I'll have our town attorney review this. In the meantime, I'm going to have to ask you gentlemen to leave Sanctuary."

"We have rights—"

"And I have a town full of people who don't take kindly to outsiders threatening one of our own." Jake's voice remains pleasant, but his eyes are steel. "You have thirty minutes to clear the town limits. My deputies will escort you."

The scouts glance around the diner, noting the hardened faces of the locals who've risen from their seats. The calculation is clear on their faces—they're outmatched.

"This isn't over," the taller one says to me. "He'll come himself next time."

They back out of the diner, the deputies following. The moment the door swings shut, my legs give way. I sink into the booth, trembling.

Ethan is beside me instantly, not touching me but close enough that his warmth reaches through my chill. "You're safe," he murmurs, low enough that only I can hear. "I won't let them take you."

Marge herself brings me a glass of water, her weathered hand squeezing my shoulder. Other patrons stop by our booth—some I recognize, others I've never met—offering quiet words of support.

"Told you," Emma says softly. "Sanctuary takes care of its own."

The drive back to the cabin passes in a blur. I stare out the window, seeing nothing, the scouts' words echoing in my head. Property. Incompetent. Omega instability. All the chains my father has used to control me since childhood.

Inside, Ethan moves cautiously, like I might shatter. He builds a fire in the hearth though the day is mild, understanding somehow that I need the warmth.

"They won't stop," I finally say, staring into the flames. "My father... he doesn't give up what he considers his."

Ethan sits beside me on the couch, leaving space between us. "Tell me."

And somehow, in the safety of his cabin with the fire crackling, I do. I tell him about growing up under Alexander Chen's iron control—pack alpha, business tycoon, tyrant. About the parade of potential alpha mates, each more repulsive than the last. About my carefully planned escape three years ago, the constant moving, the fear of being tracked down.

"Why Sanctuary?" Ethan asks when I fall silent.

A bitter laugh escapes me. "The name. Stupid, right? I thought it was just some quaint mountain town. I didn't know it would actually live up to its promise."

His hand moves slowly across the couch, palm up—an invitation, not a demand. "It will. We will."

I stare at his offered hand—calloused, strong, capable of violence and gentleness in equal measure. I should be running in the opposite direction. Instead, I place my smaller hand in his.

His fingers curl around mine, warm and steady. "My father wasn't like yours," he says quietly. "But he had expectations. Demands. The Rawlins name comes with... legacy. Responsibility." He stares into the fire. "I ran too. Just in a different way."

"And now you're back."

A small smile touches his lips. "And finding reasons to stay."

The silence that follows isn't uncomfortable. His thumb traces gentle circles on my hand, the touch so light I could break it with the slightest movement. I don't.

Outside, darkness falls over Sanctuary. In the growing shadows of the cabin, with the fire's glow illuminating our joined hands, I let myself acknowledge what I've been fighting since he carried me from the flames.

This feels like the beginning of something inevitable.

<h1 style="text-align:center">5</h1>

I wake before dawn, sheets damp with sweat, skin burning. At first, I think it's lingering trauma from yesterday's confrontation—anxiety manifesting physically. Then the telltale cramp twists low in my belly, and I know. Heat. Early, violent, triggered by stress and proximity to a compatible alpha. My father's scouts have managed to trap me after all, just not in the way they intended.

"No," I whisper into the darkness. "Not now. Not here."

My cycle has always been regular, predictable—one of the few aspects of my omega biology I've managed to control through medication and sheer force of will. I should have weeks before my next heat. But stress can override even the most carefully managed schedule, and yesterday was nothing if not stressful.

I curl into a ball, pressing my face into the pillow to muffle a groan as another cramp seizes me. The sheets against my hypersensitive skin feel like sandpaper. My rational mind is already clouding, instincts rising to the surface like a tide I can't hold back.

And the scent—Ethan's scent—saturates everything. The pillowcase, the blankets, the very air I breathe. Each inhale sends liquid fire coursing through my veins, intensifying the ache between my thighs. My body knows what it wants. Who it wants.

No. I can't stay here. Not like this.

I force myself from the bed on trembling legs, stumbling to my duffel bag. There must be suppressants in the emergency medication kit from the hospital. Something to take the edge off long enough for me to get somewhere safe. Somewhere away from him.

My fingers shake as I rummage through the bag. Nothing. Of course not—suppressants aren't standard issue. They're prescription-only, and mine burned in the fire along with everything else.

The bedroom door feels miles away. Each step sends a fresh wave of need crashing through me. I make it to the hallway, aiming for the bathroom. Cold shower. I just need to cool down, clear my head enough to call Emma.

The house is silent. Ethan must still be asleep. Small mercies. If I can just get out without him seeing me like this, smelling me like this—

The bathroom door sticks. I push harder, desperate now, and it flies open with a loud bang against the wall. I freeze, listening for movement from Ethan's room. Nothing. I slip inside, lock the door, and turn the shower to its coldest setting.

The water hits like needles against my fevered skin. I gasp, pressing my forehead against the cool tile, willing my body to obey me just this once. But the heat persists, building impossibly higher. Slick gathers between my thighs, washed away by the shower only to be replaced immediately. The empty ache inside me grows more insistent, demanding to be filled.

By him. Only him.

I bite my lip until I taste blood, fighting the urge to call his name. This isn't me. This is biology, instinct, the curse of omega physiology that I've spent my life resisting. I won't succumb now, not when I've fought so hard for my independence.

The water runs cold against my burning skin until I can't stand it anymore. I shut it off with numb fingers, wrapping myself in a towel that feels like torture against my sensitized nerves. My reflection in the mirror is a stranger—pupils blown wide, cheeks flushed, lips swollen. The scent of omega heat rolls off me in waves, unmistakable and impossible to hide.

I need to leave. Now. Before Ethan wakes.

I crack the bathroom door, listening. The house remains quiet. I dart back to the guest room, nearly crying with relief when I make it undetected. Clothes. Phone. Emma's number. That's all I need.

My fingers can't work the buttons on my borrowed shirt. I settle for the oversized T-shirt I slept in and a pair of sweatpants, wincing as the fabric slides over my skin. Every movement sends fresh pulses of need through my core. My phone screen blurs before my eyes, Emma's contact a smudge I can barely tap.

One ring. Two. Three.

"The number you have reached is not in service at this time..."

Wrong number. I try again, vision swimming, fingers slippery with sweat. The phone slips from my grasp, clattering to the floor.

"Avery?"

Ethan's voice from the hallway freezes me in place. He's awake. He's coming closer.

"I'm fine," I call out, my voice breaking on the second word. "Go back to sleep."

A pause. Then, softer: "You're not fine. I can smell—"

"Don't." The word emerges as a desperate plea. "Please, just... I need to go."

"Go where?" His voice is strained, controlled. "Avery, you're in heat."

Shame burns hotter than desire. Being an unmated omega in heat is still taboo in most circles—a failure of control, of propriety. My father's voice echoes in my memory, "Omegas who can't manage their cycles are just animals. No better than bitches in heat."

"I know what I am," I snap, anger cutting through the fog of need. "I don't need you to remind me."

Another cramp doubles me over, a whimper escaping before I can stop it. I hear him inhale sharply on the other side of the door.

"Let me help you," he says, each word measured and careful. "Not like that. I can drive you somewhere. Or call someone."

The concern in his voice nearly undoes me. No alpha has ever responded to my heat with anything but entitlement or disgust. Never concern. Never respect.

"There's nowhere to go," I admit, leaning against the door that separates us. My only barrier against what we both want. "The motel is full of tourists. The hospital would just—" I swallow hard. "They'd put me in the omega ward. Sedation and restraints until it passes."

His growl vibrates through the wood. "That's barbaric."

"That's standard procedure." My legs give way, and I slide to the floor, trembling. "It's fine. I've done it before."

The silence that follows is heavy with something I can't name. When he speaks again, his voice is closer—he's sitting on the other side of the door.

"You can stay here. I'll go."

The alpha offering to leave his own territory during an omega's heat—unheard of. Impossible. And yet he means it.

"You'd do that?" My voice sounds small, disbelieving.

"If that's what you want." No pressure. No guilt. Just a choice—mine to make.

Another wave of heat crashes through me, worse than before. I whimper, curling into myself, slick soaking through the sweatpants. His scent intensifies in response—pine and woodsmoke laced with arousal so potent it makes my mouth water.

"Ethan," I gasp, beyond pride now. "It hurts."

The doorknob rattles, then stills. "Let me in, Avery." His voice is rough with restraint. "I won't touch you without permission. I swear it."

I shouldn't. Every lesson I've learned from my father's pack, from years on the run, screams against it. Alphas can't be trusted near an omega in heat. Their biology overrides their humanity. They take. They claim. They own.

But Ethan isn't them. He's been different from the start.

With the last shred of my rational mind, I reach up and unlock the door. It swings open slowly, revealing him kneeling on the other side, his expression a battlefield of concern and desire. His pupils are dilated, his breathing ragged, but his hands stay at his sides.

The full force of his scent hits me like a physical blow. My body responds instantly, another flood of slick dampening my thighs, a moan escaping my lips. His nostrils flare, jaw clenching with the effort of restraint.

"Tell me what you need," he says, voice barely human.

What do I need? Safety. Relief. Him.

But there's more at stake than just physical release. If I give in to this heat with him, I'm choosing more than momentary comfort. I'm choosing to trust. To let someone in after years of carefully constructed walls. I'm choosing him as my alpha—biology making the decision my heart hasn't fully accepted yet.

"I need..." My voice fails me as another cramp tears through my abdomen. I reach for him blindly, fingers grasping air. "I need to choose for myself. Not because of heat. Not because of biology."

He remains kneeling just beyond my reach, trembling with the effort it takes not to close the distance between us. "Then choose," he whispers. "Whatever you decide, I'll respect it. But you need to say it, Avery. Clear and out loud."

The moment stretches between us, taut with possibility. My body screams for him, my instincts recognizing their match. But my mind—the part of me that's survived my father's control, that's built a life on my own terms—hesitates on the precipice of surrender.

Not surrender, I realize suddenly. Partnership. Ethan isn't asking me to submit. He's asking me to choose.

And for the first time in my life, the choice is genuinely mine.

6

—.—

"Yes." The word falls from my lips, quiet but certain. "I choose you, Ethan. Not the heat. Not biology. You." My fingers reach for him again, and this time I find the solid warmth of his forearm. "Please," I whisper, barely recognizing my own voice. "I need you."

Something breaks in his expression—restraint giving way to raw hunger. He moves with supernatural speed, gathering me against his chest, lifting me as if I weigh nothing. I gasp at the contact, every nerve ending sparking to life where our bodies meet.

"Are you sure?" His voice rumbles through me, vibrating in his chest where my cheek rests. "Once we start, I don't know if I can—"

"I'm sure." I curl my fingers into his shirt, inhaling his scent directly from the source. "I've never been more certain of anything."

He carries me to the bed, laying me down with surprising gentleness despite the tremors I feel running through his powerful frame. His eyes are almost all pupil now, the ring of amber barely visible. They track my every movement as I reach for the hem of my sweat-soaked shirt.

"Let me," he murmurs, his large hands replacing mine.

The shirt slides over my head, the cool air a blessed relief against my burning skin. Ethan's sharp intake of breath as he takes in my naked torso sends a fresh wave of slick between my thighs. I should feel exposed, vulnerable. Instead, I feel powerful. Wanted.

"You're beautiful," he says, voice reverent. His fingertips hover just above my skin, not quite touching. "So beautiful it hurts to look at you."

I reach for his hand, guiding it to my breast. The contact shatters whatever remaining control he's been clinging to. He groans, a sound more animal than human, and lowers his mouth to capture mine in a bruising kiss.

His taste explodes across my tongue—pine and smoke and something uniquely him that my omega recognizes on a molecular level. Right. Mine. Alpha. I open for him instinctively, letting him claim my mouth as his hands explore my body with increasing urgency.

My sweatpants disappear, along with his clothes. I barely register the movements, lost in the sensation of skin against skin, the delicious weight of him pressing me into the mattress. The emptiness inside me intensifies to a desperate ache, my body producing enough slick to soak the sheets beneath us.

"Need you," I pant against his mouth. "Now, Ethan. Please."

He hovers for one suspended instant, eyes searching my face, then his mouth claims my throat, teeth scraping just enough to make me shudder with anticipation. "I'll take care of you," he promises. "Always."

Every touch is a question: Will you let me? Do you want this? When I arch my neck for him, signaling yes, his hand slides possessively around my waist, pinning me with ease. I want to fight it, on principle, out of years of hard-won autonomy. But my body overrides my rebellion, melting beneath his weight, desperate for contact. I feel the press of his cock, thick and hot against my thigh, but he ignores his own need, intent only on the wreckage he's making of me.

He moves lower, lips skimming beneath my ear, tongue flicking at the pulse point until I gasp and writhe for more. My legs part instinctively, slick coating my inner thighs as my heat climbs from fever to inferno. I'm shaking, breathless, so wound up I can't distinguish embarrassment from craving. That's when he lands a trail of open-mouthed kisses down my collarbone, pausing to bite at the slope of my shoulder. His growl vibrates against my skin, equal parts hunger and restraint.

He never breaks eye contact unless he's worshipping my body. There's a power in it, that deliberate attention, as if he's reading every microexpression, every involuntary twitch. Down my sternum, he teases at my nipple with his tongue, swirling and sucking until I'm moaning, greedy hands threading through his hair and dragging him closer. The sensation is overwhelming. Every nerve ending lit, every thought dissolved in pure, animal need.

He's slow at first, almost cruel, circling my areolae before nipping gently at the peaks, then laving away the sting. My hips buck upward, seeking friction, but he holds me pinned, refusing to let me rush. "Patience, omega," he murmurs, voice gravelly with command. "Let me take care of you." The words shouldn't inflame me the way they do, but they go straight to the ache between my legs, doubling my desperation.

He travels lower, mouth and hands mapping the planes of my belly, pausing to tongue my navel, then easing my thighs apart with a reverence that borders on worship. The cool air makes me hyperaware of how soaked I am, slick pooling beneath me, scent thick enough to choke the room.

"So perfect," Ethan mutters, like he can't believe his luck, and I flush at the awestruck note in his voice.

His mouth pauses just above my mound. I can feel his breath, hot and humid, as he inhales my scent deeply. The alpha's pupils are blown wide, almost feral, but he waits for another sign of permission. I can't speak, so I whimper and cling to his shoulders, angling my hips up, offering. That's all it takes for him to dive in, tongue parting my folds with a hunger so honest it steals my breath.

The first stroke is light, exploratory, but when he finds my clit he latches on with devastating precision, sucking and rolling the tender flesh until I'm sobbing with relief. I clutch at his head with both hands, grinding against his face, uncaring of shame or dignity. He brings one massive hand up, spreading me wider with his thumbs, exposing me even further to his relentless attention.

Every lap of his tongue is a shockwave, a direct transmission from my cunt to my brainstem, scrambling my thoughts into static. I'm aware only of the exquisite torture, the building pressure, the way he hums into me when I moan his name. My thighs threaten to snap shut around his ears, but he holds me open, devouring me with single-minded focus. When he slides a finger inside, thick and careful, curling just so, I nearly black out.

He senses my impending release and doubles down, tongue working in ruthless tandem with his fingers, never letting up for a second. My body bows off the mattress, muscles seizing, nails digging welts into his scalp. For a split second, time fractures, and I hover at the edge, suspended between agony and ecstasy.

The first orgasm hits with stunning force, my body convulsing around nothing, the emptiness still unbearable despite the momentary relief. Ethan works me through it, relentless, drawing out every aftershock until I'm gasping his name like a prayer.

"Alpha," I whimper, the word slipping out unbidden. "Need you inside."

Something changes in his scent—sharpens, deepens. His eyes flash as he moves back up my body, positioning himself between my thighs. I feel him, hot and hard against my entrance, the head of his cock slipping through the abundant evidence of my arousal.

"Mine," he growls, the sound vibrating through my bones.

"Yours," I agree, the word feeling like truth rather than submission. "And you're mine."

His control snaps. He drives into me with a single powerful thrust, stretching me to the point of delicious pain. I cry out, nails digging into his shoulders hard enough to break skin. He stills instantly, concern breaking through the haze of rut.

"Did I hurt you?" His voice is strained, the effort of not moving clearly costing him.

I shake my head, adjusting to the perfect fullness of him inside me. "Don't stop. Please, don't stop."

The relief in his expression is palpable. He begins to move, each thrust precise and devastating, hitting places inside me I didn't know could feel pleasure. My heat-heightened senses register every detail—the salty taste of his skin when I press my lips to his neck, the tension in his muscles as he holds back from taking me too roughly, the musky scent of our combined arousal filling the room.

"More," I demand, wrapping my legs around his waist to draw him deeper. "I won't break."

His rhythm falters, then accelerates. He braces one arm beside my head, the other sliding beneath me to tilt my hips at a new angle that tears a scream from my throat. Each thrust now hits a spot that sends white-hot sparks shooting up my spine.

"That's it," he growls against my ear. "Let me hear you. Let me feel you come apart."

The second orgasm builds faster than the first, coiling tight at the base of my spine before exploding outward in waves that leave me shaking. I clench around him, drawing a harsh groan from his chest. His thrusts grow erratic, powerful, almost desperate.

I feel it then—the base of his cock beginning to swell, catching slightly on my entrance with each thrust. His knot. The biological lock that will bind us together through the peak of my heat and his rut.

"Please," I gasp, surprising myself with the urgency of my need to be knotted, claimed completely. "Give it to me."

Ethan's eyes lock with mine, something vulnerable and fierce in their depths. "You're sure?"

"Completely."

With a roar that seems torn from his very soul, he drives in one final time, his knot swelling to full size, locking us together as his release floods me in hot pulses. The sensation triggers a third climax that steals my breath, my vision going dark at the edges as pleasure beyond anything I've experienced crashes through me.

We collapse together, Ethan careful to roll to his side without separating us, his knot still pulsing inside me. He gathers me against his chest, his heartbeat thundering beneath my ear. His hand strokes down my sweat-slicked back in gentle, soothing motions.

"Are you okay?" he murmurs against my hair, his voice rough with emotion.

I nod, too overwhelmed to speak. The heat hasn't broken—it won't for at least another day—but the desperate edge has dulled, replaced by a warm contentment I've never felt before. Our scents have merged, creating something new and intoxicating that marks us as a bonded pair.

"I never thought I'd find you," Ethan says quietly. His hand comes up to cup my cheek, tilting my face to meet his gaze. "My whole life, I've felt... incomplete. Even coming back to Sanctuary, something was missing. It was you, Avery. It's always been you."

Tears burn behind my eyes. In my father's pack, omegas were possessions—valued for breeding potential and status, not as individuals with their own worth. But the way Ethan looks at me now contains no hint of ownership, only awe and tenderness.

"I ran for so long," I whisper against his chest. "I thought I was running from bonds, from being controlled. I didn't realize I was running toward you."

His arms tighten around me. "I won't ever cage you. I swear it."

I believe him. That's the miracle of it—after years of distrusting every alpha I've met, I believe him without reservation. Biology plays its part, but this is something deeper, something that transcends instinct.

His knot begins to ease, but he makes no move to separate us. Instead, he traces patterns on my skin, his touch reverent. "I will protect you," he vows, voice low and fervent. "From your father. From anyone who would try to claim you against your will. You are mine to cherish, not to control."

The words settle into my bones, a promise more binding than any pack law. For the first time in my life, belonging to someone doesn't feel like captivity—it feels like freedom.

"My heat isn't over," I warn him, already feeling the embers rekindling as the first wave subsides.

He smiles against my temple, his hand sliding down to rest possessively on my hip. "Good. Because I'm nowhere near done showing you exactly what it means to be mine."

The claiming repeats throughout the day and night—sometimes frantic and primal, sometimes slow and tender. We break only for water, for moments of rest curled together like wolves in a den. With each joining, something inside me shifts and settles. The fear that's been my constant companion for years recedes, replaced by a certainty I've never known.

I've found my sanctuary. Not in a place, but in a person.

In the brief moments of clarity between heat waves, I wonder if my father will still come for me.

If the battle for my freedom is truly over or just beginning.

But with Ethan's scent merged with mine, his claim written on my body inside and out, I find I'm no longer afraid. For the first time in my life, I'm not facing the fight alone.

7

My heat breaks on the third day, leaving Ethan and me exhausted but irreversibly bonded. His scent has become part of mine, a permanent marker that announces to any alpha with functioning nose receptors that I am claimed. Taken. Protected. The bond settles between us like a living thing, a constant awareness of each other that borders on telepathy. When he returns to his shift at the fire station, I feel the distance like a physical ache, but not the desperate panic I'd feared. This bond strengthens rather than weakens me—a revelation that contradicts everything my father taught about omega attachments.

A week passes in domestic bliss that should feel suffocating but somehow doesn't. The cabin becomes truly ours rather than his with me as guest. My clothes hang beside his in the closet. My favorite tea appears in the kitchen cabinet. We discuss finding a bigger place eventually, but neither of us feels any urgency to leave this sanctuary where we found each other.

The warning comes on a Tuesday morning. Emma calls while I'm preparing for my first shift back at the hospital.

"Avery, stay home today." Her voice is tight, controlled. "Call the hospital. Tell them you're sick."

A chill runs down my spine. "What's happening?"

"Your father." She pauses, and I hear voices in the background. "He's here. In Sanctuary. With a pack lawyer and three enforcers."

The mug slips from my fingers, shattering on the kitchen floor. Ceramic shards scatter across the tile like my fractured sense of security.

"How do you know it's him?"

"Jake intercepted them at the town limits. They're demanding a meeting. With you. In one hour."

My legs give way. I sink to the floor amidst the broken ceramic, barely feeling a shard slice into my palm. "Where's Ethan?"

"On his way to you. Jake's stalling them." She hesitates. "Avery, the whole town is mobilizing. You're not alone in this."

The words barely register through the roaring in my ears. Alexander Chen doesn't negotiate. He doesn't request. He takes what he believes is his, consequences be damned.

"I'll be ready," I hear myself say before hanging up.

Ethan arrives in a screech of tires on gravel, bursting through the door with wild eyes and disheveled hair. He finds me still on the floor, surrounded by broken ceramic, blood dripping from my palm.

"Avery." My name on his lips sounds like a prayer and a curse combined. He kneels before me, taking my injured hand in his. "Emma called you?"

I nod, unable to speak.

"We don't have to do this," he says, pressing a kitchen towel to my cut. "We could leave. Right now. I have savings. We could go anywhere."

The offer tempts me—running has been my solution for three years. But a new certainty takes root in my chest, blooming outward.

"No," I say, my voice steadier than I feel. "I'm done running."

His expression shifts from concern to fierce pride. "Then we face him together."

The town square buzzes with tension when we arrive. It seems all of Sanctuary has materialized on this Tuesday morning, forming a loose perimeter around a cluster of black SUVs with out–of–state plates. Sheriff Jake stands at the center of the square, flanked by deputies. Emma waits nearby, her face tight with worry.

And then I see him—Alexander Chen, pack alpha, business tycoon, my father. He hasn't changed in three years. Still immaculately dressed in a tailored suit that screams wealth and power, silver streaking his dark hair in distinguished patterns. The three men surrounding him are clearly enforcers—massive alphas with the dead-eyed look of those who follow orders without question.

A smaller man in wire-rimmed glasses clutches a briefcase—the pack lawyer, no doubt.

Ethan's hand tightens around mine as we approach. I feel his restrained fury through our bond, the protective rage barely contained beneath his calm exterior. Jake nods to us, relief flashing across his face.

"My daughter." My father's voice carries across the square, silencing the murmurs of the gathered crowd. "At last."

I step forward, forcing my spine straight despite the instinctive urge to cower before my former alpha. "Father."

His nostrils flare as he scents the air between us. Something dark crosses his face. "You've allowed yourself to be claimed by this... local."

"I've chosen my mate," I correct him, the words coming easier than I expected. "My alpha."

"A firefighter," he sneers, dismissing Ethan with a contemptuous glance. "A nobody from nowhere. After everything I've invested in you. The education. The connections. The suitable matches I arranged."

"You mean the alphas you tried to sell me to," I retort, shocking myself with my boldness. "The business arrangements where I was the commodity."

"You are pack property!" His mask of civility cracks, revealing the tyrant beneath. "Omega offspring belong to the pack. That is our law."

"Not our law," Jake interjects, stepping forward. "Not in Sanctuary."

My father's cold gaze shifts to the sheriff. "Your backwater town ordinances don't supersede pack law. The Jade Mountain pack has standing in three states."

"Not this one." Jake's voice carries the full weight of his authority. "In Sanctuary, we recognize individual autonomy regardless of designation."

The pack lawyer clears his throat nervously. "We have documentation proving the omega's legal attachment to the pack, signed by her when she was seventeen."

"Coerced signatures from minors don't hold up here," Emma calls out, her voice ringing clear across the square. Other voices join hers, a chorus of support that swells around us.

My father's face darkens with rage. "This is absurd. She is my daughter. My blood."

"I am my own person," I say, stepping forward until only a few feet separate us. Ethan moves with me, his solid presence at my back giving me strength. "I left your pack legally when I turned twenty-one. I filed the separation papers. I followed protocol."

"Papers I never signed," he counters.

"Papers you didn't need to sign. Check your laws again." The months of research, of working with omega rights advocates, shine through my words. "A pack alpha's signature is only required for omegas under twenty-one or those judged mentally incompetent by a neutral medical board."

Uncertainty flickers across the lawyer's face. My father notices and turns on him with a snarl.

"She's right," the lawyer admits reluctantly. "The incompetency claim was our workaround, but it requires medical evaluation before removal—"

"She's unstable," my father interrupts. "Running away. Living like a vagrant. Working menial jobs when she was raised for greater things."

"I'm a registered nurse," I correct him, heat rising in my cheeks. "I save lives. I build something rather than destroying it, which is more than I can say for you."

A ripple of approval runs through the crowd. My father's enforcers shift uneasily, glancing around at the growing number of Sanctuary residents gathering in the square. They're outnumbered, and they know it.

"You've bonded with this man without my approval," my father says, his voice dropping to a dangerous register. "That alone is grounds for pack intervention."

"She doesn't need your approval," Ethan speaks for the first time, his voice steady but thrumming with protective rage. "Avery chose me. I chose her. The bond is legal and registered with the state as of yesterday."

My father's eyes widen in genuine shock. "You registered the bond?"

"With the county clerk," Jake confirms, a hint of satisfaction in his tone. "It's official and binding. Any attempt to separate a legally bonded pair is a federal offense, pack law notwithstanding."

The lawyer tugs urgently at my father's sleeve, whispering something in his ear. My father shakes him off, his face contorted with barely contained fury.

"This isn't over," he growls. "Bonds can be broken. Registrations challenged."

"Not this one." I take a final step forward, close enough to see the flecks of gray in his dark eyes—eyes so similar to my own. "I am no longer your daughter, and I am certainly not your property. I am a citizen of Sanctuary.

This is my pack now." I gesture to the people surrounding us—Emma and Jake, the diner owner, the general store clerk, nurses from the hospital, firefighters from Ethan's station. "These people are my family."

Something flashes in my father's eyes—hurt, perhaps, buried instantly beneath cold rage. "You'll regret this choice," he says softly. "When he tires of you. When you realize what you've thrown away for a temporary infatuation."

"It's not infatuation." Ethan's arm slides around my waist, anchoring me as our scents merge in the air between us—proof of a bond my father can't deny. "It's mate recognition. Something you wouldn't understand since you've never experienced it."

The barb hits home. My father's loveless arranged marriage is common knowledge in our former pack—a business merger sealed with a mating ceremony.

"We're done here," I say with finality. "Leave Sanctuary. Don't come back."

"Or what?" My father's lip curls.

"Or we'll make you leave." Jake steps forward, hand resting on his holster. Around the square, Sanctuary residents move closer, a unified front of determination.

My father's gaze sweeps the crowd, calculating odds. Finally, he buttons his suit jacket with a sharp tug.

"This isn't over," he repeats, but the threat sounds hollow now. "The Jade Mountain pack doesn't forget betrayal."

"Neither does Sanctuary," Emma calls back.

He turns on his heel, gesturing curtly to his enforcers and lawyer. They pile into their sleek vehicles, engines growling to life with unnecessary aggression. As the SUVs pull away from the square, a collective breath releases from the gathered crowd.

Someone starts clapping. Others join in until applause surrounds us. Ethan's arm tightens around my waist, his lips pressing against my temple.

"You were magnificent," he murmurs against my skin.

I turn in his embrace, searching his face. "He'll be back. Or he'll send others."

"And we'll be waiting." The certainty in his voice matches the iron resolve I feel solidifying in my own chest. "Together."

The crowd disperses slowly, people stopping to offer support, to introduce themselves, to welcome me properly to Sanctuary. Emma hugs me fiercely, whispering congratulations. Jake shakes Ethan's hand, something unspoken passing between the brothers.

Standing in the town square with Ethan's scent wrapped around me like armor, I realize a fundamental truth: I've spent three years running from my father, but what I've really been running toward is this—a place where I'm valued for myself, not my designation. A community that fights for its own. A mate who sees me as an equal, not a possession.

I've found my pack. My true family.

8

— · —

I wake tangled in Ethan's arms, his steady heartbeat under my ear, his scent wrapped around me like the softest blanket. Dawn light filters through the curtains, painting golden stripes across the rumpled sheets. For a moment, I simply exist in this bubble of safety—this perfect moment where my alpha's warmth keeps the world at bay. Then yesterday crashes back into focus—my father in the town square, the confrontation, the entire town of Sanctuary standing with us. Standing with me. The enormity of what happened, of what I've claimed for myself, hits like a physical blow.

Ethan stirs beneath me, his arms tightening instinctively. Even in sleep, he responds to my distress. The bond between us pulses, new and raw and powerful.

And therein lies my fear.

How much of this is real? How much is simply biology—alpha instincts responding to omega need? Yesterday, facing down my father, the entire town rallied behind us. Behind me. But would they have done so if I weren't mated to a Rawlins? If I weren't carrying Ethan's scent?

My father's words echo, "When he tires of you. When you realize what you've thrown away for a temporary infatuation."

Ethan's eyes open slowly, immediately finding mine. A sleepy smile curves his lips before he registers the tension in my body.

"What's wrong?" His voice is rough with sleep, concern instantly replacing contentment.

"Nothing." The lie tastes sour.

He props himself up on one elbow, searching my face. "I can feel your anxiety through the bond, Avery. Talk to me."

I pull away slightly, needing space to think clearly without his scent clouding my judgment. "Yesterday was... a lot."

"Your father won't come back," he says, misunderstanding my concern. "Not after that public rejection. His pride won't allow it."

"It's not that." I sit up fully, drawing the sheet around me despite our intimacy. "It's... us. This." I gesture vaguely between us.

His brow furrows. "What about us?"

The words stick in my throat, but I force them out. "What if this isn't real? What if it's just biology? Instinct? What if you woke up one day and realized you've tied yourself to someone you barely know because of a scent and a heat?"

Pain flashes across his face. "Is that what you think happened?"

"I think..." I swallow hard, staring at my hands twisted in the sheets. "I think the town defended me because I'm yours. I think you defended me because your alpha instincts can't help but protect a bonded omega. I think we're both caught up in something that happened so fast we haven't had time to question it."

Silence stretches between us. I force myself to look up, expecting anger, perhaps even agreement. Instead, I find Ethan watching me with infinite tenderness.

"May I touch you?" he asks quietly.

The formality of the request surprises me. I nod.

He takes my hands in his, his touch gentle but grounding. "The first time I saw you, you were unconscious in a burning building," he begins. "My job was to get you out safely. That was instinct, training, duty. Nothing more." His thumbs trace circles on my palms. "But the moment I carried you outside, when you opened your eyes and looked at me—that wasn't just biology, Avery. That was recognition."

I start to speak, but he shakes his head.

"Let me finish. Did our scents trigger something primal? Yes. Did your heat and my rut accelerate a process that might otherwise have taken months? Absolutely." His hands tighten slightly around mine. "But that doesn't make it less real. It just means our bodies recognized what our hearts would have discovered anyway."

"How can you be so sure?" I whisper.

"Because I've met hundreds of omegas in my life and never once felt what I feel with you." His voice drops, intimate and fierce. "Because I came back to Sanctuary feeling incomplete and only started feeling whole when you entered my life. Because I would have stood between you and your father even if we'd never shared a heat, never bonded, never shared more than a conversation."

Something loosens in my chest—a knot of fear I've been carrying since yesterday. Since my heat broke, if I'm honest with myself.

"The town defended you because they saw your worth," he continues. "Emma befriended you before we bonded. Jake offered protection when you were just a fire victim. Sanctuary claimed you as its own before I ever did."

"And if it doesn't last?" The question escapes before I can stop it—my deepest fear laid bare.

Ethan's expression softens further. "Then I'll still be here," he says simply. "If you wake up one day and decide this isn't what you want, I won't hold you captive with a bond. We'd figure it out." He brings my hands to his lips, pressing a kiss to my knuckles. "But I'll spend every day proving that this is real. Not just pheromones and instinct, but a choice I make each morning."

Tears burn behind my eyes. No one has ever offered me both devotion and freedom in the same breath.

"What about children?" I ask, voice barely audible. "A house? A future? We haven't discussed any of that."

A slow smile spreads across his face. "I want it all with you. Children with your eyes and stubborn spirit. A bigger house at the edge of town—room for a family but close enough for you to reach the hospital easily. Years of watching you grow more magnificent than you already are." He pauses. "But only if and when you're ready. There's no rush, Avery. We have time."

The tears spill over. "I'm scared," I admit. "Not of you. Of this feeling. It's too big. Too much. I don't know how to trust it."

"Then don't trust the feeling yet," he says, reaching up to brush away a tear with his thumb. "Trust me instead. Trust yourself. The feeling will prove itself with time."

I lean into his touch, the last of my resistance crumbling. "I do trust you. That's what terrifies me."

He pulls me gently against his chest, his scent enveloping me in safety and warmth. I go willingly, my body molding to his as if designed for this purpose.

"We'll take it one day at a time," he murmurs into my hair. "Today, tomorrow, next week. No pressure. No expectations beyond what feels right."

I nod against his chest, soaking in his certainty until it begins to feel like my own. We stay like that, wrapped in each other and the quiet morning light, until the shrill ring of his phone shatters the moment.

Ethan reaches for it with a sigh, keeping one arm firmly around me. "Rawlins," he answers. His body tenses as he listens. "Where?... How many?... I'm on my way."

He hangs up, already shifting into professional mode. "Chemical spill on the highway. Truck overturned. They're calling in everyone."

"Go," I say, pulling back to give him space. "I understand."

He's already moving, pulling on clothes with practiced efficiency. "Should be back by dinner, but I'll text if it runs long."

A thought strikes me as he heads for the door. "Wait. Do they need medical support? The hospital will be sending ambulances, but if there are multiple injuries..."

Ethan pauses, considering. "They didn't mention medical, but it's still developing. Why?"

"I'm coming with you." I'm already out of bed, reaching for my clothes. "I'm a nurse, Ethan. This is what I do."

"It could be dangerous—"

"So is an ER on Saturday night." I pull a shirt over my head, decision made. "I won't get in the way of the fire response. But I can help triage until more ambulances arrive."

He watches me dress, something like pride and surprise mingling in his expression. "You sure?"

"Positive."

A slow smile spreads across his face. "Then let's go."

I grab my kit while he snatches up water bottles and protein bars from the kitchen counter. Our movements mirror each other—quick, purposeful, without collision.

In the truck, he thumbs the radio and tells dispatch I'll be joining as a medical responder. "Avery's an ER nurse, three years trauma experience," he says, and something in his tone—pride without possession—makes my chest tighten in a way that has nothing to do with adrenaline.

As we speed toward the accident scene, sirens clearing our path, I realize something profound has shifted between us. This morning I woke afraid that our bond was built on biology alone—alpha protecting omega, instinct overriding reason.

Now, racing toward danger side by side, each bringing our own skills to help strangers in need, I understand what we truly are: partners. Equals. A team formed not despite our designations but beyond them.

For the first time since my heat broke, since my father appeared in town, since I chose Ethan as my mate, I feel completely certain.

This is real. This is right. This is us.

And I'm no longer afraid of any of it.

9

— • —

The Sanctuary Festival transforms the town square into something magical—paper lanterns strung between buildings, food stalls lining the perimeter, a wooden dance floor erected in the center where couples already sway to the local band's country melodies. Two weeks have passed since the confrontation with my father, two weeks of settling into life with Ethan, of truly becoming part of Sanctuary rather than just existing within its borders. Still, my stomach knots with nerves as we approach the festival entrance. Public events were forbidden in my father's pack unless carefully choreographed to enhance his status. The chaos and joy of a small-town celebration feels foreign, almost dangerous in its freedom.

"You okay?" Ethan's hand settles at the small of my back, warm and grounding.

I nod, leaning into his touch. "Just... taking it all in."

He studies my face, reading me with the eerie accuracy our bond provides. "We don't have to stay long if it's overwhelming."

"No," I say firmly. "I want to be here. I want this."

His smile crinkles the corners of his eyes. "Then let's get you some of Marge's famous apple pie before the line gets ridiculous."

We step into the festival grounds, and I'm immediately struck by how different this feels from my last public appearance. The night of the fire, I was a stranger pulled from flames. During the confrontation with my father, I was a contested omega at the center of a territorial dispute. Tonight, I'm simply Avery—Ethan's mate, Sanctuary resident, part of the fabric of this place.

People greet us with easy familiarity—firefighters from Ethan's station, nurses from my hospital shifts, the clerk from the general store who still blushes when Ethan buys me anything feminine. No one stares at our joined hands or the visible bond mark on my neck. Here, our pairing is already accepted as natural, inevitable.

"Avery!" Emma waves from a picnic table where she sits with Jake and several other couples. "Come sit with us!"

Ethan raises an eyebrow in question. I nod, and we thread our way through the crowd.

"You look gorgeous," Emma declares, scooting over to make room. She's right—the simple sundress I'm wearing is nothing special, but Ethan's appreciative gaze all evening has made me feel beautiful in a way no expensive outfit ever did.

"Thanks for talking me into the dress," I tell her, settling beside her while Ethan heads to the beer tent with Jake.

"It's nice to see you relaxing finally," she says, nudging my shoulder. "You've been wound tight since the day you arrived in Sanctuary."

"Had reasons to be," I remind her.

"And now?"

I watch Ethan at the beer tent, laughing at something Jake said, his head thrown back in genuine mirth. My heart swells. "Now I have reasons not to be."

The evening unfolds in a blur of sensory pleasures—sweet-tart apple pie that lives up to its reputation, Ethan's arm draped casually around my shoulders, dancing awkwardly on the wooden platform until we find our rhythm together, strings of lights reflecting in his amber eyes as night falls.

Around nine, the music stops. Mayor Collins, a weathered beta with a voice that carries without shouting, steps onto the makeshift stage.

"Welcome, friends, to the 63rd annual Sanctuary Festival!" Cheers erupt from the crowd. "As tradition dictates, we've reached the time for new bond acknowledgments."

My stomach drops. Ethan tenses beside me.

"I didn't know," he murmurs. "We don't have to—"

"What is it?" I whisper back.

Emma leans in from my other side. "It's just a Sanctuary tradition. Newly bonded pairs can publicly acknowledge each other. Totally optional."

Three couples move toward the stage, all looking nervous but happy. The mayor beams at them. "First, the Hendersons—newly wedded last month!"

The crowd applauds as a young beta couple takes the stage, sharing a chaste kiss.

"Next, the Wilsons—celebrating fifty years together this summer!"

An elderly alpha and omega couple join the first pair, the crowd cheering louder for their longevity.

"And the Patels—welcoming twins next spring!"

More applause for the glowing expectant parents.

"Any other bonds to acknowledge tonight?" the mayor asks, scanning the crowd.

Ethan's hand finds mine, squeezing gently. "Your call," he says quietly. "No pressure."

In my father's pack, bond acknowledgments were performative displays of dominance—alphas parading their omegas like trophies, emphasizing submission and ownership. The thought of participating in anything similar makes my skin crawl.

But the couples on stage don't look dominated or controlled. They look... happy. Equal. Celebrated rather than evaluated.

I squeeze Ethan's hand back. "Let's do it."

His eyes widen in surprise, then soften with something that makes my heart stutter. Without a word, he leads me toward the stage. A murmur passes through the crowd as we approach—the firefighter and the nurse, the alpha who defied an outside pack for his mate.

"Ah!" The mayor's face lights up. "Ethan Rawlins and Avery Chen! Come up, come up!"

We climb the short steps to the wooden platform. Ethan's hand never leaves mine, his thumb tracing soothing circles on my palm.

"Tradition allows the alpha to speak first," the mayor explains to me with an apologetic shrug. "Old customs die hard, even in Sanctuary."

I brace myself, unsure what to expect. In my father's pack, this would be the moment for an alpha to declare ownership, to emphasize the omega's submission to pack hierarchy.

Ethan steps forward, but instead of addressing the crowd as expected, he turns to face me directly. He takes both my hands in his, his eyes never leaving mine.

"Avery," he begins, his voice quiet but carrying in the sudden hush. "I acknowledge you not as mine to possess, but as my equal to cherish." A surprised ripple runs through the audience. "I offer you my protection without demanding your submission. My strength without requiring your weakness. My love without expecting your surrender."

Tears blur my vision. This isn't the traditional acknowledgment. This is something new—something revolutionary in its simplicity.

"I promise to stand beside you, not in front of you," he continues, his voice growing stronger with each word. "To listen when you speak. To support your dreams as fiercely as my own. To remember always that our bond was formed by choice, not capture." His hands tighten around mine. "You are not my possession. You are my partner. My mate. My heart."

A tear slips down my cheek. Ethan releases one hand to brush it away, his touch infinitely tender.

The mayor clears his throat, visibly moved. "And you, Avery? Do you wish to acknowledge your bond?"

Words fail me. Instead, I reach up to frame Ethan's face with my hands and pull him down for a kiss that says everything I can't articulate. The crowd erupts in cheers and whistles. Against his lips, I finally find my voice.

"I acknowledge you as my chosen alpha," I whisper for his ears alone. "The one who showed me that strength lies in connection, not isolation. That freedom can exist within commitment. That love doesn't have to cage."

His forehead rests against mine, our breaths mingling. "Thank you for choosing me."

"Every day," I promise. "I'll keep choosing you every day."

The mayor ushers us off stage, the band strikes up again, and we're swept into a tide of well-wishers. Emma hugs me fiercely, whispering congratulations. Jake claps his brother on the shoulder, something like pride in his eyes.

In a brief lull between conversations, I glance toward the festival entrance—and freeze. A familiar figure stands at the perimeter, watching. My father. Not approaching, not threatening, just... observing.

Ethan follows my gaze, his body instantly tensing. "Want me to have him removed?"

I consider it, then slowly shake my head. "No. Let him see."

"See what?"

"What he never understood." I turn in Ethan's arms, my back to my father, focusing on the man who taught me what love should actually be. "What he could never give me."

As we sway gently to the music, I sense my father watching. Let him see how Ethan holds me—securely but without restraint, treasured without being trapped. Let him witness how an alpha and omega can exist in harmony rather than hierarchy. Let him observe what happens when love replaces control.

When I glance back toward the entrance minutes later, he's gone. No confrontation. No final threats. Just quiet acknowledgment of defeat.

A weight lifts from my shoulders—not just the fear of my father's interference, but the burden of isolation I've carried for years. Looking around at the festival, at the community that rallied around me, at the man who holds me like something precious, I finally understand. I haven't lost my independence by accepting connection. I've strengthened it.

The lone wolf isn't the strongest member of the pack. The strongest are those in the center, supported on all sides, drawing power from their bonds rather than being diminished by them.

"What are you thinking?" Ethan murmurs against my hair as we dance.

"That I spent three years running from the wrong thing," I admit. "I was so afraid of being controlled that I cut myself off from being supported."

His arms tighten around me. "You found your way here eventually."

"To Sanctuary."

"To home," he corrects gently.

The word settles in my chest, warm and right. Home. Not a place, but a feeling. Not walls, but arms that hold me. Not silence, but laughter shared with friends who've become family.

The festival lights sparkle overhead like stars brought down to earth, illuminating the community that's become mine. The music swells around us, and for the first time in my life, I surrender completely—not to an alpha or a pack, but to the simple, profound joy of belonging exactly where I am.

10

—·—

The cabin glows with golden light when we return from the festival, welcoming us home in a way that feels newly significant. Ethan holds my hand as we climb the porch steps, both of us quiet, content to exist in the gentle aftermath of the evening. Inside, the space that once felt like his territory now reads as ours—my books on the coffee table, my throw blanket on the couch, my scent mingled with his in every room. Not his home with me as a guest. Our home, created together.

"Want tea?" Ethan asks, shrugging out of his jacket.

I shake my head, stepping closer to him instead. "Not tea."

His eyes darken as he reads my intention.

His hands find my waist, pulling me against him with delicious restraint. The bond between us hums with anticipation, desire feeding desire in an endless loop. I rise to my tiptoes, press my lips to the hollow of his throat where his pulse hammers beneath the skin. "I choose you," I whisper against his warmth. "Again. Now."

Ethan groans, the sound vibrating through both our bodies. His fingers tangle in my hair, tilting my face up to his. "Every day," he murmurs, echoing our promise from the festival. "I choose you every day."

The kiss ignites something primal between us—not the desperate, biology-driven need of my heat, but something deeper, more deliberate. A claiming that comes from choice rather than instinct. His tongue sweeps into my mouth, and I taste the sweetness of festival desserts and something uniquely him beneath it. My hands find the buttons of his shirt, fumbling with urgency.

"Here?" he asks against my lips, already backing me toward the kitchen counter. "Or upstairs?"

"Start here," I gasp as his teeth find my earlobe. "Finish wherever."

His laugh is dark chocolate and whiskey, rich and intoxicating. He lifts me onto the counter in one fluid motion, stepping between my spread thighs. The sundress rides up, exposing skin still golden from the evening sun. Ethan's hands slide up my bare legs with agonizing slowness, thumbs tracing circles just shy of where I want them.

"Festival's got me thinking," he says, voice rough as his fingers hook into the waistband of my underwear. "About all those traditions. Bond acknowledgments. Public statements."

I lift my hips, letting him slide the fabric down my legs. "And what conclusion did you reach?"

His eyes meet mine, amber darkening to molten gold. "That some things are better celebrated in private."

The counter is cool against my heated skin as he pushes the dress higher, exposing me completely to his hungry gaze. I should feel vulnerable, exposed. Instead, I feel powerful—goddess to his worshipper. I reach for his belt, tugging him closer.

"Show me," I challenge.

The belt buckle hits the floor with a metallic clang. His jeans follow, pooling around his ankles. He kicks them aside, never breaking eye contact. My hands slide beneath his unbuttoned shirt, mapping the contours of his chest, feeling his heart thundering beneath my palm.

"I love you," he says simply.

The words pierce me more deeply than any touch. Three words we've danced around but never explicitly stated. Heat floods my cheeks, and something tightens in my chest.

"I love you too," I whisper, the truth of it catching in my throat.

He lifts me as if I weigh nothing, and I clutch his shoulders, legs winding around his hips in greedy, animal claim. Ethan's hands span my back, spines of his fingers splayed wide as he pins me flush against his chest and strides for the stairs. The house blurs around us—sofa, lamp, entry rug, all irrelevant and abandoned to the hunger curling between us. My lips mark a lightning path along his jaw, tasting salt and sun and the wild hint of char from the festival bonfire still clinging to his skin. His beard scrapes, his mouth opens, and we nearly crash into the wall but neither of us slows.

We lose pieces on the way up: my dress snared mid-thigh, riding higher and higher until the hem threatens scandal with every step; his shirt half-unbuttoned, then ripped open as I yank at him in frustration, sending buttons skittering across the hardwood like dice cast in a game only we know how to play. I arch against him, nails digging into the planes of his back, and Ethan's growl is so deep I feel it echo in my bones. He nips my collarbone and I gasp, reveling in the bite—proof that we are here, alive, and together.

Halfway up, my body turns molten, slick with anticipation. He pauses just long enough to press me against the banister, hands kneading my ass with proprietary intent, and the pressure is so exquisite I moan shamelessly into his hair. His scent floods my senses, pure Alpha, but it's different now—no longer overwhelming, but a call and answer to my own, the two of us mingling in the air. Ethan's pupils are huge, all hunger, but his gaze never lets go of mine, pinning me to the present, to this moment, to him.

My dress is shed somewhere near the top stair, left behind like a flag of surrender. Ethan shoulders open the bedroom door—our bedroom, I finally let myself admit—and the hush inside is electric. The air is heavier here, charged with everything we've said and everything we haven't. He sets me down, slow and reverent, but my hands are already moving, impatient with the zipper on his jeans. He laughs, breathless and wrecked, and helps me as we stumble backward onto the bed in a tangle of limbs and laughter.

We're naked before I know it. Not just bare, but stripped of the last armor we wore around our hearts. His skin is hot and damp, his body a map I want to memorize with tongue and teeth and fingertips. I devour him—shoulders, chest, down the line of muscle to where I can feel his need for me, rigid and real against my thigh. My own body is desperate, aching, and when his hand slides between my legs it's all I can do not to come undone right there.

But he waits. He always waits for me. He kisses my temple, gentle, then my eyelids, then the edge of my mouth.

I answer with my whole body, arching to meet him, wrapping him in my arms, pulling him down so there's no space left between us at all. I want him to know I'm not just giving in. I'm choosing this, choosing him, every day, every second.

The bed welcomes us with a soft creak. Ethan hovers above me, his weight braced on powerful arms, giving me space to breathe, to choose, to want. Always careful, always mindful of my need for freedom within intimacy. I reach up to trace the lines of his face—the strong jaw, the slight crinkle at the corners of his eyes, the mouth that knows exactly how to unravel me.

"Don't hold back," I tell him, arching up to brush my breasts against his chest. "I won't break."

Something shifts in his expression—restraint giving way to raw desire. He captures my wrists in one large hand, pinning them gently above my head as his mouth blazes a trail down my neck, across my collarbone, to the swell of my breast. When his teeth graze my nipple, I cry out, back bowing off the mattress.

"So responsive," he murmurs against my skin. "So perfect for me."

His free hand slides between my thighs, finding me slick and ready. One thick finger circles my entrance, teasing, testing, before pressing inside. A second follows, stretching deliciously. My hips rise to meet each thrust of his hand, seeking more, deeper, harder.

"Please," I gasp, beyond pride or patience. "I need you inside me."

He releases my wrists, braces himself above me. The blunt head of his cock nudges where his fingers just were. Our eyes lock as he pushes forward, a single smooth thrust that seats him fully inside me. The stretch burns perfectly, my body welcoming him as if designed for this purpose.

"Mine," he growls, beginning to move.

"Yours," I agree, nails digging into his shoulders. "And you're mine."

The rhythm builds between us, a relentless tide that drowns out everything else. The mattress rocks beneath us, each thrust pushing me further toward a precipice I've never fallen from without reservation, without fear. Ethan's body is a weight, a warmth, a universe focused on me. His hips drive into mine, his hands cage my wrists above my head, but there's nothing trapping about it; it's a surrender I give freely, a tether that grounds me, makes me real.

He moves with purpose—no hesitation, no holding back—like he wants to memorize me from the inside out. Every inch of him fits me perfectly, stretches me to the edge of pain, then soothes it with a roll of his hips, a kiss at my throat, a murmured "you're so good for me" against my skin. I can't breathe, can't think, except for the relentless, perfect friction and the knowledge that I'm wanted like this, wholly, not just for my ability to take care or to survive, but for who I am in this moment—with him, for him.

I wrap my legs around his waist, ankles locking. He groans at the change in angle, the new tightness, and the sound is so raw it vibrates through my ribs. His cock hits that spot inside me, the place that makes my vision go white at the edges. I arch up, urging him deeper, and Ethan's lips find my jaw, teeth grazing my chin as if he needs to mark me in every way he can.

He moves faster. The slap of our bodies is loud in the room, primal. The scent of us—slick, sweat, Alpha and Omega—saturates the air, heady and intoxicating. I'm lost to it. He lifts my hips and drives harder, and the first flickers of heat begin to spark in my belly, a slow-building fire that promises annihilation.

"Let go, Avery," he rasps, eyes black with want. "Don't hold back. I want all of you."

His hand leaves my wrist to cup my cheek, thumb stroking the sweat-damp skin. I turn into his palm, baring my throat in automatic submission, and the sight of it pulls a sound from him that's almost a snarl. He bends down to bite gently at the soft skin just below my ear, not breaking the flesh, just enough pressure the claiming mark.

My body answers, a surge of need so sharp I almost sob. My nails rake his back, dragging him closer if that's even possible, and my hips buck up to meet every thrust. The bedframe creaks a protest, and for a crazy second I hope it collapses, sends us tumbling to the floor tangled together, because I want this memory burned into the wood and the carpet and the drywall, proof that we existed like this.

"Look at me," he says, voice low and rough. "I want to see you."

It's a command, but not a demand. I force my eyes open, meeting his gaze as the first waves of orgasm begin to crest. The intensity of his stare—possessive without owning, loving without diminishing—pushes me over. I come with his name on my lips, clenching around him, pulling him deeper.

"That's it," he groans, his thrusts becoming erratic. "Come for me, Avery. Show me how good we are together."

The aftershocks still ripple through me when he follows, his release hot inside me, his body shuddering with the force of it. He collapses beside me rather than on me, always mindful, always careful even in abandon.

We lie tangled together, heartbeats gradually slowing, sweat cooling on our skin. Ethan's fingers trace idle patterns on my stomach, raising goosebumps in their wake. The bond between us pulses, sated but alive.

"You've ruined me for solitude," I say into the comfortable silence.

He props himself up on one elbow, studying my face. "Is that a complaint?"

"An observation." I turn to face him, our noses almost touching. "I used to think independence meant being alone. Standing apart. Now I understand it's about having the freedom to choose connection."

His smile crinkles the corners of his eyes. "And you choose this? Us?"

"Every day," I echo our promise. "But I still want my career. My identity beyond being your mate."

"I'd expect nothing less." His hand cups my cheek. "The hospital offered you that trauma coordinator position, didn't they?"

I nod. "More responsibility. Better hours. A chance to develop the emergency response protocols for the whole county."

"You should take it." No hesitation, no calculation of how it might impact him or us. Just support, clean and simple.

"And you?" I ask. "Jake mentioned the fire chief is retiring next year."

A shadow crosses his face. "I'm not sure I want the administrative headache."

"But you'd be brilliant at it. The station respects you. The town trusts you." I trace his bottom lip with my thumb. "You could implement all those training programs you're always talking about."

"Maybe." His expression softens. "We have time to figure it out. Both of us."

The simplicity of that statement washes over me like warm water. Time. A future stretching before us, unrushed and full of possibility. Not the frantic escape I've been living for years, not the careful isolation I'd accepted as the price of freedom.

"We should get a bigger place," I say sleepily. "Somewhere with more rooms. For the future."

His eyes darken with understanding. "Children?"

"Someday." The word doesn't terrify me as it once did. "When we're ready."

He pulls me closer, tucking my head beneath his chin. I feel his heartbeat against my cheek, steady and strong. "No rush," he murmurs into my hair. "We have a lifetime."

Sleep begins to claim me, warm and inevitable as the tide. Just before I drift off, I realize what feels different about tonight compared to all our previous nights together. For the first time in my life, I don't feel owned or controlled.

I feel chosen.

And I've done the choosing too.

Inside, in the warmth of our bed, I've finally found what the town promised in its name—a place of safety, of acceptance, of belonging.

Not because I was rescued from flames by an alpha firefighter. But because, for the first time in my life, I've stopped running long enough to be found.

Find out what happens next in Sanctuary with Silas and Annabelle's story in The Alpha Rancher! (Continue to the next page for a Bonus Epilogue.)

Want more of Ethan and Avery? Sign up for the Ash Jade newsletter and download a free bonus scene today! Click here: The Alpha Firefighter Bonus Scene

BONUS EPILOGUE

ANNABELLE

The scent of fear clings to my skin as I stuff Mia's worn teddy bear into the backpack. My fingers tremble, catching on the zipper. Outside, voices rise and fall like thunder—the alpha's rage a storm gaining strength, and somewhere beneath it, a scent that matches mine. Family. Pack. My chest tightens. This time, the lightning will strike us all.

"Annie?" Mia whispers from the corner bunk, her small face half-hidden in shadow. "Are we in trouble?"

I force my lips into what I hope passes for a smile. "Just a little adventure, sweet girl."

The communal hall stretches dark around us, moonlight filtering through the high windows to paint silver squares on the wooden floor. I've chosen this hour carefully—most packmates sleeping, night guards patrolling the perimeter rather than the buildings. Still, every creak of the old structure sends my pulse racing.

Liam's shoes. Mia's medicine. Three changes of clothes each. The cash I've hidden beneath the loose floorboard, saved penny by penny from mending clothes for the pack elders. Not enough. Never enough. But it has to be.

A crash outside makes me flinch, followed by a snarl that vibrates through the walls. Alpha Reese's voice carries like a blade.

"Where the fuck is she?"

My body responds before my mind can catch up—neck baring instinctively, a whimper building in my throat. I bite down on my lip until I taste blood. Not this time. Not with the children at stake.

"I don't know, sir." It's Beth, our pack's beta female. The lie in her voice is subtle, but I catch it—she knows exactly where I am. She bought me this time, this slender chance.

Something shatters. Glass, maybe a bottle. "Don't lie to me. I can smell her heat coming."

Heat. The word sends a flush of panic through me. Three days away, by my estimate, but the signs are there—the restlessness, the heightened scent, the ache building low in my spine. Perfect fucking timing, as always. I swipe sweat from my forehead and move faster.

"Liam," I whisper, nudging my brother's shoulder. At twelve, he's all gangly limbs and too-serious eyes. "Time to go, buddy. Just like we practiced."

He doesn't ask questions, just slides from the bottom bunk and reaches for his boots. I love him for it—for understanding without making me explain.

My hand brushes against the inside pocket of my jacket, finding the folded paper with Beth's cousin's address. Sanctuary. A town where omegas can claim independence, where pack law bends to individual choice. A fairy tale, probably. But right now, fairy tales are all we have.

"What belongs to me stays with me." Alpha Reese's voice drops lower, more dangerous. "The pups, the omega—they're mine by pack law. You think I don't know she's planning something? You think I don't know about the car?"

Ice floods my veins. The car—our escape route, borrowed from the pack mechanic who owes me for keeping quiet about his illegal brew operation. If Reese knows about that—

"We have to go. Now." I zip the backpack with a decisive tug and sling it over my shoulder. "Mia, your coat. Liam, help your sister."

Seven-year-old Mia scrambles from her bed, eyes wide but movements silent. We've rehearsed this too many times to count, always as a game. The quiet game, I called it. Whoever makes a sound loses. Tonight, losing means something altogether different.

"Mine!" The roar outside is followed by the splintering crack of wood—a door or fence giving way to alpha strength. "Annabelle! Show yourself!"

My name on his lips makes my omega nature curl in on itself, instincts warring between submission and flight. He's not calling me as my alpha; he's calling me as property. The distinction clears my head.

Three months since our parents' accident. Three months of watching Reese's interest in me shift from indifference to possession, of intercepting the way his gaze follows Mia with speculation about her future designation, of noticing how he assigns Liam the most dangerous chores despite his age. Three months of planning, saving, waiting for the right moment.

I pull Mia's coat around her small shoulders and check the window. The commotion has drawn packmates into the yard—shadows moving in torchlight, voices raised in question or protest.

"They're sending hunters," I mutter, more to myself than the children. Through the glass, I watch four of the pack's strongest betas gather around Reese, nodding at whatever instructions he's giving. My stomach turns. Those aren't just any betas—they're trackers, wolves who can follow a scent through rain and snow and darkness.

"Are they going to hurt us?" Mia asks, clutching her coat closed.

I kneel before her, hands on her shoulders. "No. No one is hurting either of you ever again. But we need to be very, very quiet now. Like mice."

She nods solemnly. "Like the quietest mice ever."

"Exactly." I kiss her forehead, breathing in her sweet pup scent for courage. Then I turn to Liam. "Back door, through the kitchen, straight to the toolshed. Don't stop for anything."

His jaw sets in a hard line. "I can protect us."

"I know you can." The lie tastes bitter. He's brave, my Liam, but he's still a child against grown predators. "But tonight, protecting means running. Fast."

A howl cuts through the night—the traditional call before a hunt. My time has run out.

We slip from the sleeping quarters into the kitchen, keeping to the shadows. Each footstep seems to echo, each breath too loud. The smell of dinner still lingers—venison stew, eaten hours ago while I smiled and nodded and pretended I wasn't counting the minutes until escape.

My heat scent will give us away if we linger. Already I can feel the first tendrils of it rising through my skin, responding to stress and fear. Another evolutionary joke at omega expense—danger triggers hormones triggers heat triggers vulnerability. A perfect cycle of fucked.

The back door squeaks on its hinges. I freeze, but the noise outside masks the sound. Cold air rushes in, carrying the scent of pine and snow and something else—something I can't place. Something alpha, but not from our pack. The scent is distant but distinct—earth and smoke and something sharp like citrus. It cuts through my fear for just a moment, making my omega stir in curiosity rather than dread.

I push it away. No time for distractions.

"Go," I whisper, nudging the children through the doorway. The three of us dash across the open yard between the hall and the toolshed, exposed under the night sky. My heart hammers against my ribs, expecting a shout, a spotlight, a hand closing around my arm.

We make it. The toolshed door closes behind us, plunging us into darkness broken only by the thin beam of my flashlight. The smell of motor oil and rust surrounds us.

"Wait here," I breathe, easing past stacked boxes toward the shed's rear wall. My hands find the tarp, pulling it back to reveal our salvation—a dented blue sedan, ancient but functioning. I slide into the driver's seat and push the key into the ignition, praying to whatever deity might be listening.

The engine coughs, sputters, and catches with a growl that seems deafening in the small space. No time for subtlety now.

"In! Quick!" I lean over to unlock the passenger door. Liam scrambles in first, then pulls Mia onto his lap. "Seatbelts," I remind them automatically, as if we're just going for a Sunday drive.

The large shed doors should open automatically with the button on my keychain, but they stick halfway. Of course they do. I should have checked, should have tested—

"Annie," Liam's voice is tight with fear. "They're coming."

Through the gap in the doors, I see them—five figures running toward the shed, Reese in the lead. His face contorts with rage when he sees the car, the children, me behind the wheel.

"MINE!" The word isn't even human anymore, just animal fury given voice.

I slam my foot on the accelerator. The car lurches forward, crashing through the half-open doors with a shriek of metal. Mia screams. Liam holds her tight. I keep my eyes fixed ahead as we bounce down the dirt track that leads away from the pack compound.

In the rearview mirror, I see Reese drop to all fours, beginning to shift. The betas follow suit, bodies contorting as they prepare to chase us on four legs instead of two. A wolf can outrun a car on these mountain roads. I've always known that. The only advantage we have is head start and direction.

The car fishtails as we hit the main road, tires skidding on the mix of dirt and early winter frost. I correct, hands white-knuckled on the steering wheel, and push the old engine harder than it's been pushed in years.

"Are they following?" I ask, unable to look back again.

Liam twists in his seat. "Yes. Lights behind us."

"Truck," Mia adds, her voice small.

Not wolves then—at least not yet. They've opted for vehicles first. Smart. They'll save their energy for when the chase leads off-road, which it inevitably will. There's only one route out of pack territory, and they know I know it.

I take a hard right onto a service road that cuts through the forest. Not the route to Sanctuary, not yet. First, I need to lose them, to make them think we've gone north toward the interstate when we actually need to go east.

The sedan bounces over ruts and rocks, every impact jarring my teeth. Mia whimpers with each bump, but Liam keeps his arms around her, steady and strong beyond his years.

"It's okay," I tell them, the lie automatic. "We're going to be fine."

The wind shifts as we climb higher into the foothills, and that's when I catch it again—that unfamiliar alpha scent, stronger this time. Male, powerful, but somehow not threatening. It pulls at something deep in my omega hindbrain, a recognition that makes no sense. I've never met this alpha. I'd remember that scent—like the forest after rain, like woodsmoke from a hearth, like safety.

Impossible. No alpha means safety. I know better.

Yet as I steer us toward the fork in the road, some instinct I can't name pulls me east rather than north. East, where that scent seems to originate. East, where Sanctuary supposedly waits. East, where a strange alpha's territory intersects with our desperate flight.

"Where are we going?" Liam asks, noticing the turn.

"Somewhere safe," I answer, hoping it's true.

Behind us, headlights appear and then fade as the truck following us continues north, taking the bait of our false trail. Relief floods me, but I know it's temporary. They'll realize their mistake soon enough. Wolves always do.

I press harder on the gas, willing the car's ancient engine to give us more speed. The mountain looms ahead, its slopes dark against the night sky. Somewhere on the other side lies

Sanctuary—and apparently, the source of that compelling scent.

Find out what happens next for Silas and Annabelle in The Alpha Rancher!

ALSO BY ASH JADE

Read more from Ash Jade
Short, binge–worthy omegaverse romances where
instinct burns hot and love always wins.

Lost Ridge Riders Universe

Welcome to Lost Ridge.
*Where the roads are long, the walls are guarded,
and no omega is ever owned—only chosen.*

Salt and Timber Coast Universe

Welcome to the Salt & Timber Coast.
A rain-bound peninsula where protection is steady, bonds are chosen, and love means staying.

Blackwater Bears

A quiet inland pack where bear shifters offer shelter, endurance, and a home that holds.

The Starfall Ridge Quick Reads Series

Welcome to Starfall Ridge.
Where the crater sparks scents, fate strikes fast, and no one escapes the pull of a mate.

The Yule Curse Series

Four fated nights. Four cursed alphas. One winter where heat burns brighter than fire.

The Touch Her and Die Series

In a world ruled by dominance, instinct, and the pull of fate, every story begins with danger—and ends with devotion.

<u>The Sanctuary Pack Series</u>

Welcome to Sanctuary.
*A hidden mountain town where omegas come to
heal—and alphas learn what it means to protect.*

ABOUT ASH JADE

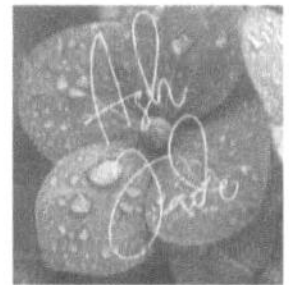

Ash Jade writes trope-packed omegaverse romances full of heat, ruts, and fated mates — but always with heart. Her stories are fast, messy, and addictive, blending primal passion with emotional cores that make the bonds hit even harder. If you love bingeable romances where instinct tangles with feelings (and always ends in happily-ever-after), you've found your pack.

ashjadeauthor.com